A Rainbow Bridge for Gus

Written by Barbara Bareis Rigabar
Illustrated by Chris Sharp
Layout by Ashley Delgado

Gracie ran to the window and looked out. The rain had finally
stopped. She had been waiting all day to go on a bike ride with
her dad. "Now, Daddy? Now?" she asked.

This book is a gift for

Westridge Elementary Library,

and tail wags,

Barbara Rigail

Dedicated to our sweet, lovable Gus, and all the animal friends who show us how to love each other unconditionally.

"Where every tail has a story

A Rainbow Bridge for Gus A Story about the Loss of a Pet,
Published by Lovable Tails, LLC Wildwood, MO 63038.
For more information visit: www.lovabletails.com
ISBN-13: 978-0615924762
ISBN-10: 061592476X

Library of Congress Control Number: 2013922366
Copyright 2013 Barbara Bareis Rigabar

Cover design and illustrations by Chris Sharp
Interior Layout by Ashley Delgado
Edited by David Mead

A portion of the proceeds from this book go to the Association for Pet Loss and
Bereavement dedicated to caring for those who have lost a companion animal.

Printed in the United States of America

Gracie's dad smiled, "Yes!" he said.
"And we can take the two-seater bike."

"Alright!" Gracie cheered as she hopped up and down. She ran to get
her jacket and helmet.

It wasn't long into their ride when an excited Gracie
pointed toward the clearing sky. A beautiful rainbow
stretched across the horizon. She smiled and shouted,
"Look, Daddy, a rainbow! It's so pretty."

Gracie's dad looked up,
"It looks like Gus's rainbow, the one we saw
after he went to heaven, doesn't it?"

"Ooh, it does," Gracie said with a smile.
"Gus was the best dog."

Gracie and her dad rode to the park where they had
so often come to play with Gus. They parked their bike
and sat on the bench. Soon they began sharing favorite
stories about their family dog.

"Remember," Gracie started, "when Gus was a puppy and got his nose stuck in the bag of chips? When he finally shook the bag loose, there were chips everywhere!" she giggled.

"Then he stole my peanut butter and jelly sandwich," her dad laughed. "What a mess! Yep, Gus was a handful from the very beginning."

"I'll never forget the first time we took him swimming at the lake," Gracie's dad recalled. "I splashed into the water and called for him to come to me. But instead, I ended up falling in! Gus just sat on the bank staring at me. I think he was laughing!"

"Oh, and remember when he got loose at the vet's office? He chased the other dogs and cats around and knocked everything over," Gracie said as she hid her big smile.

"Or when he snatched Mom's shoe and ran off with it right before we were going out for dinner," her dad added. "I chased Gus around the front yard trying to grab that shoe out of his mouth!

"Even when Gus got into trouble, we couldn't stay mad at him. One look at his funny face was all it took. Soon we were petting and hugging him, telling him that he was a good dog,"
Gracie's dad reminded her.

"We had so much fun together," Gracie said.

"You and Gus were the best of pals," her dad recalled. "When you were little, he went everywhere you went. He was so patient and gentle when you climbed all over him, and he was always there when you needed a friend to play with. In the backyard pool, he was your lifeguard. And sometimes he even let you win at tug of war."

"Yeah, but not too often," Gracie chuckled.

"I loved how he always ran to meet me at the bus after school and the way he snuggled me with his cold, wet nose. But my favorite thing to do with him was to dress him up, especially at Halloween! Remember the ghost costume?" Gracie giggled.

"That was so funny!" Gracie's dad laughed. "You know, I think Gus really enjoyed it."

Then there was a long pause.

"But then Gus got older, and he didn't want to run and play anymore. I was sad when that happened, but he still wagged his tail when I cuddled with him on his bed," Gracie said softly.

"Well, Gracie, that's just part of life," her dad quietly explained. "Gus was such a silly puppy at first. Then he grew to love all the wonderful things that made up his life, especially being a part of our family. As he got older he walked slower and slept more. The vet told us that Gus was very old. Finally his body just wore out and he died. It was time for Gus to cross the Rainbow Bridge into heaven."

Gracie scooted closer to her dad and hugged him. "I remember when we said goodbye to Gus," Gracie said with a sad look.
"It was right here at his favorite park."

"Yes, I remember how Gus licked our faces as we told him we would love him forever and would see him again one day," Gracie's dad said softly. "And we made a print of his paw," Gracie sniffled. "Something we could keep forever."

"And then...just a little while later...it was time. Gus went across the Rainbow Bridge," her dad explained.
"Now God is taking care of him."

"I was so sad when Gus left us," Gracie said with teary eyes.

"Me too," he said. "It's sad for us because we miss Gus so much, but it's not so sad for him. I like to think of Gus across the Rainbow Bridge in heaven. He isn't old and tired or sick anymore. Gus is healthy and happy. He has lots of friends to play with there."

"Right after we said goodbye to Gus at the park, we saw a beautiful rainbow, remember? I know it was Gus's Rainbow Bridge!" She said with excitement.

Gracie's dad smiled.

"Now when I see a rainbow, I'll remember how much I loved Gus. He will always be in my heart," she grinned.

As the sun began to set, Gracie and her dad climbed back on their bike. "Daddy, it feels good to talk about Gus and remember how much fun we had." Gracie said as they rode together.

"Yes, Gracie, it makes me feel good, too,"
her dad warmly replied.
"Gus will always be in our hearts and a part of our family."

The End

Rainbow Bridge

Cut along dotted line

On this day,_____ left our loving arms and waits for us on the Rainbow Bridge where we will be together someday.

Please use this space to create a special "Memory Page" of your pet.
You may draw a picture, create a photo collage,
or write a letter to your pet on the space provided.
For more information visit: www.lovabletails.com

About the loss of a family pet...

When our dog, Gus, died we struggled with how to talk to our young children about it. After all, this was their first experience with death. Shortly thereafter, I read a touching poem about the "Rainbow Bridge". It described a loving place where pets went after they died and where we would someday be reunited with them. This poem inspired me to share our family's story.

After a loss, parents should acknowledge the sadness children are experiencing and encourage them to express how they feel. It is important for children to see that grief is a normal reaction to loss. For many children their pets were a best friend and a model of unconditional love and loyalty. It will be difficult for them to cope with loss. Drawing a picture of their pets or writing a letter to them are activities that may provide comfort. There is a special activity at the end of this book to help children remember the unique place their pets had in their lives.

Additional resources can be found at:

The Association for Pet Loss & Bereavement:
www.aplb.org

Barbara Barais Rigabar

About the Author

Barb Rigabar wrote her first book, *A Rainbow Bridge for Gus*, to celebrate the unique bond a family has with a loved pet. The book was based on her family's story about their dog, Gus. Barb lives in Wildwood, Missouri with her family and dog, Tucker. Learn more at: www.lovabletails.com

About the Illustrator

Chris Sharp has been illustrating children's books for over thirty years, having illustrated over two-hundred titles. He is a co-owner of Smart Kidz Media. Married with five children and twelve grandchildren, he is still the biggest kid in the house. He lives in St.Charles, Missouri.